ALL OF A SUDDEN A BOY ABOUT their age dressed in dirty, torn clothes came running toward them. He came up close to Gracie and ripped the locket from her neck. Then he took off, zigzagging through the crowds.

The girls started screaming. *"Au secours!* Help! Someone, please, help!!!"

Without even thinking, Rosemary Rita dropped her bag, hiked up her skirt, and raced after the boy.

"I wish I wasn't wearing these stupid boots," she panted.

Her hat went flying off and her curls flapped in the breeze. She was a fast runner and the boy wasn't expecting a chase.

Rosemary · In · Paris

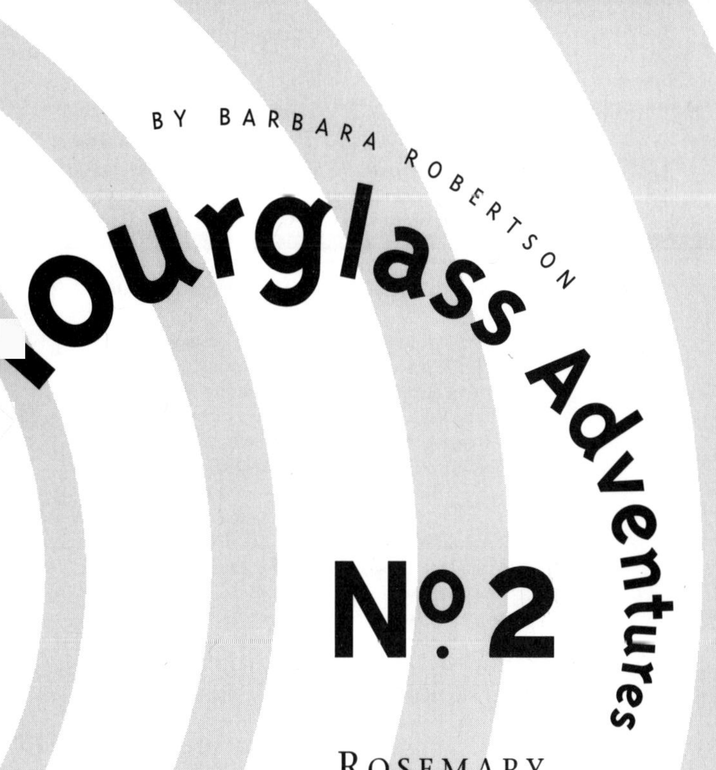

Rosemary In Paris

WINSLOW PRESS
FLORIDA NEW YORK

Library of Congress Cataloging-in-Publication Data
Robertson, Barbara
Rosemary in Paris / by Barbara Robertson.—1st ed.
p. cm.—(The hourglass adventures; #2)
Summary: Rosemary Rita's magical hourglass takes her
to the Paris Exposition of 1889, where she meets
her great-great-grandmother Gracie, also aged ten,
and together with a friend they set out to catch
the boy who steals Gracie's locket.
ISBN: 1-890817-56-2
[1. Great-grandmothers—Fiction. 2. Grandmothers—Fiction.
3. Magic—Fiction. 4. Time travel—Fiction.
5. *Exposition universelle de 1889* (Paris, France)—Fiction.
6. Paris (France)—History—1870–1940—Fiction.] I. Title.

PZ7.R54466 Ri 2001
00-043457 [Fic]—dc21

Creative Director
Bretton Clark

Editor
Margery Cuyler

Designer
Annemarie Cofer

PRINTED IN THE UNITED STATES OF AMERICA
First edition, 05/01

WINSLOW PRESS

Discover *The Hourglass Adventures*' interactive Web site with worldwide links, games, activities, and more at winslowpress.com

HOME OFFICE
770 East Atlantic Avenue, Suite 201
Delray Beach, FL 33483

ALL INQUIRIES
115 East 23rd Street, 10th Floor
New York, NY 10010

To my Mother and Father,
with gratitude for all their love
and support.

Rosemary · In · Paris

Adventure Nº 1

Rosemary Meets Rosemarie

On her tenth birthday, Rosemary Rita receives ten packages from her grandmother. The boxes have been passed down through the generations, from Rosemary to Rosemary. Now it's Rosemary Rita's turn to discover the magic inside them. Among the antique postcards, clothing, trinkets, and special objects, she discovers an unusual hourglass. She flips it over while reading the oldest postcard, and suddenly she's transported back more than 130 years to Berlin, Germany! There she meets her ten-year-old great-great-great-grandmother, Rosemarie Berger. The two girls decode the secret message that's on the postcard, which leads to the release of a famous German writer who has been taken prisoner in France during the Franco-Prussian War. Rosemary Rita has a wonderful time with her great-great-great-grandmother—until she realizes she might be trapped in the past forever. But the hourglass, when flipped again, returns her to the present, where only one hour has passed.

Rosemary Rita can't wait to go on another adventure....Read on!

Chapter 1

The · Hourglass

THE SUN WAS RISING above the nearby mountaintops in Greenville, South Carolina, when Rosemary Rita woke up. The clock on her bedside table read 6:02 A.M. Rubbing her eyes, she groaned, pulled the covers over her head, and tried to go back to sleep. Today was the second day of her spring break, and she had been looking forward to sleeping late. But after five minutes of tossing and turning and twisting the sheets into a knot, she gave up.

Rosemary Rita fluffed her pillow and leaned back. As she

stared at the ceiling, a thought occurred to her. The hourglass! Quickly throwing off the covers, she scrambled out of bed and darted over to her desk. She had to make sure that the hourglass was still there. After shuffling through some homework papers and magazines, she spied it. "Phew," she sighed, picking up the antique hourglass. As she rubbed her fingers along the wooden stand, touching the ridges of the scene etched into the end, she thought of all that had happened yesterday. Meeting her great-great-great-grandmother. The bustling streets of Berlin. The excitement of figuring out the hidden message in the postcard.

Suddenly, a loud shriek came from across the hall. It was Rosemary Rita's two-year-old brother, Ryan. Heavy footsteps plodded by her door. "Mom to Ryan's rescue," thought Rosemary Rita.

Carefully, she placed the hourglass back on her desk and went to brush her teeth. Pulling her straight brown hair away from her face, she checked her tiny nose for any new freckles. Satisfied that the freckle count had remained the same, she continued getting ready. Reaching for a washcloth, she accidentally knocked over the bubblebath. Goopy purple soap spread across the sink and dripped to the floor. The flowery scent reminded Rosemary Rita of Mimi, her grandmother, who always smelled like lilacs.

Rosemary Rita was desperate to go wake her grandmother, who was sleeping downstairs. Yesterday, after Mimi showed up for a surprise visit, she told Rosemary Rita the story of when she discovered the hourglass. She too had been ten years old. She had casually turned it over while reading an old postcard and BINGO! she had been whisked back in time to the 1889 World's Fair in Paris. Now Rosemary Rita wanted to go, too. She just had to find out more. Racing downstairs, she bounded to the guestroom where her grandmother was sleeping and barged in without knocking. Mimi sat up in bed, blinking sleepily. She looked at Rosemary Rita and took a deep breath.

"Oh, it's you, dear. You startled me."

"Sorry I woke you, but I'm dying to talk

to you. We need to start planning my next adventure right away!"

Mimi reached over to the nightstand, found her glasses, and put them on. She smoothed her auburn hair with her fingers. "All right," she said sleepily. "How about some breakfast first? I can't think on an empty stomach."

"Oh, Mimi, I'm too excited to eat!" exclaimed Rosemary Rita.

"Skip breakfast? Out of the question. You've got to have something! Honey, go upstairs and get dressed. Then we'll eat and plan our day. We need to prepare carefully for your next journey."

Rosemary Rita sighed. "Okay. But after breakfast, we can get started, right?"

"Yes, dear. Now run along."

Rosemary Rita raced up the steps two at a time to her bedroom. She hurriedly ran a comb through her straight brown hair. Then she pulled her tan jeans over her long skinny legs and threw on a white shirt and a purple sweater. As she was putting on her tennis shoes, she let out a yelp. "Ouch!" she cried. There was a blister on her heel from the tight-laced leather boots she had worn yesterday as she tromped around Berlin.

Rosemary Rita was almost out the door when the gleam from the golden locket caught her eye. It was one of the many objects she had unpacked yesterday when ten boxes from Mimi had arrived for her birthday. She had sent them from New York before showing up for a surprise visit. Along with the hourglass, everything in the boxes had belonged to the generations of Rosemarys who had come before her. Rosemary Rita snatched the locket from under one of the boxes, stuck it in her pocket, and raced downstairs. Dad had already left for work. Mom, Ryan, and Mimi were at the kitchen table eating pancakes and bacon. Rosemary Rita blinked at them in surprise. They hardly ever had breakfast together. Usually Rosemary Rita ate a cup of dry cereal in the car with Dad on the way to school. But with no school and Mimi visiting from New York, Mom was making a special effort. Pancakes the size of silver dollars were piled high on her plate. A little plastic cup filled with syrup was perched next to them.

Rosemary Rita smiled at her mom and sat down. "My favorite breakfast," she said. "Mimi should visit more often!"

Mom smiled. "I agree!"

"I sticky, Mama," cried Ryan, holding out his gooey fingers. Mom lifted Ryan out of the high chair. As she tried to wipe his hands, he put them on his head, rubbing the syrup through his hair.

"Ew, gross!" said Rosemary Rita.

"I'm taking Ryan upstairs for a bath. He's wearing his breakfast!" said Mom, lifting him onto her hip and leaving the kitchen.

Rosemary Rita turned to Mimi and whispered, "Do you have the Paris postcard we looked at yesterday?"

"I certainly do," she said, pulling it out of her pocket. "Would you like me to read it to you again?"

"Oh, yes, please," Rosemary Rita said. Her heart gave a flutter as she waited for her grandmother to start.

Mimi cleared her throat. "It's addressed to Miss Rosemary Grace Christianson, your great-great-grandmother. She's the daughter of the Rosemary that you met yesterday. Her family nicknamed her Gracie because of her middle name. Just like your mom goes by her middle name, Leigh."

Mimi translated the words from French to English as she read.

June 12th, 1889

Dear Gracie,

I can't believe we are finally going to meet face-to-face. Did you get my package? Please wear the locket so that I will know it's you.

On June 19th we will both be at the Exposition. I'll wait for you in front of the Eiffel Tower. Be there at 10:00 A.M.

Your friend,

Sophie

Post It!:

Visit the postcard gallery and make your own card at winslowpress.com

Rosemary Rita reached into her pocket and pulled out the broken locket. "Mimi, this locket has got to be the one that Sophie mentioned. I wonder how it broke. Tell me again what happened when you went back in time."

"Well, as I told you, I didn't get to stay long. When I first arrived, I was standing at the base of the Eiffel Tower. I walked down a path lined with statues until I came to a giant bronze dome. I wish I could remember all the details on the buildings. There were lots of remarkable things—lions' heads, garlands, crowns, and statues that looked like they came from ancient Rome. I saw the Palace of Machines and the Palace of Fine Arts. They were huge and grand, as if they had been built for kings, queens, and emperors. But before I even got to meet your great-great-grandmother, I flipped the hourglass over by accident and came back to the present."

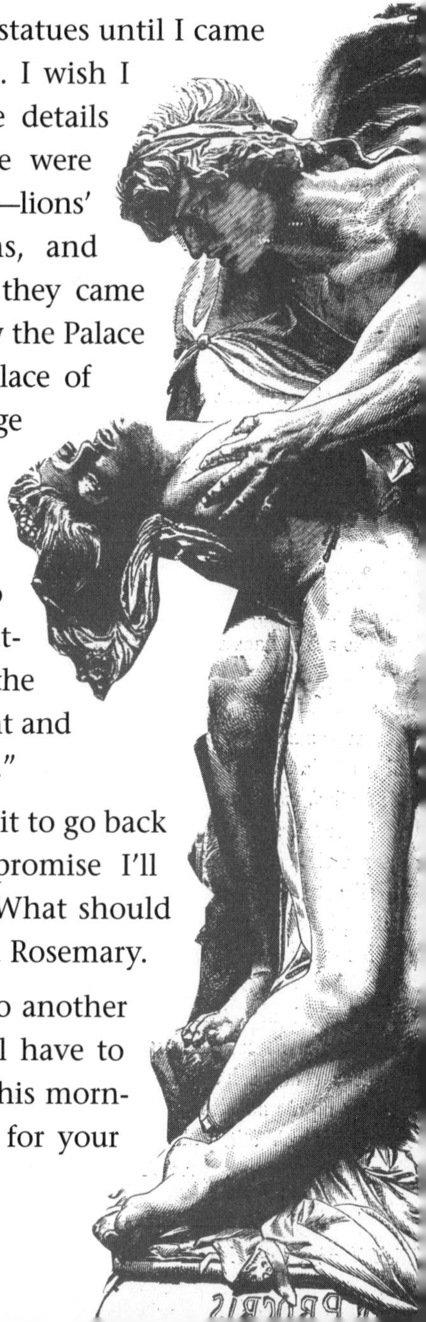

"That's why I can't wait to go back to the same place. I promise I'll remember every detail. What should I do to get ready?" asked Rosemary.

Mimi helped herself to another heap of pancakes. "We'll have to make a couple of stops this morning to get you outfitted for your trip. First, we'll go to Costume Curio on Laurens Road. It's important that you dress like the other girls did in the 1880s. Then we'll shop for a special bag to hold the hourglass and the other things you'll need in Paris."

"Ooh, this is so exciting! Let's go," squealed Rosemary Rita.

Chapter 2

Shopping · With · Mimi

IN JUST A FEW MINUTES, THEY were in the car driving to the costume store. Mimi parked in front of Costume Curio, and Rosemary Rita jumped out. The saleslady buzzed them in. She had on a black suit with a fake fur collar and red-rimmed glasses that matched her shoes. Little rhinestones sparkled around the frames of her glasses. "May I help you?" she asked.

After Mimi explained what they needed, the saleslady ushered them past a section devoted to Southern belles. Finally they came to a rack marked EUROPE, 19TH CENTURY. "This store sure has everything," observed Rosemary Rita.

Costume Shop:

Dress up Rosemary Rita
at winslowpress.com

Mimi sifted through the hanging clothes and pulled out two dresses. The first one was a blue-and-white striped dress with a long waist and buttons running down the front. Mimi held it up to Rosemary Rita. "I'm afraid this is too small, dear. Let's look at the other one." She held up the navy-and-green plaid dress with a high velvet collar and fitted jacket. The bottom of the skirt was pleated, and there was a sash around the waist. "Perfect," said Mimi. "Now, we need to find a matching hat."

"No, we don't! We already have one. It's the green velvet hat you sent in one of the packages. I tried it on last night. It looks like it was made to go with this dress," said Rosemary Rita. She twirled around the rack, holding the dress in front of her.

Mimi smiled. "Let's see, we've got the dress and the hat. That just leaves your boots."

Rosemary Rita groaned. "Do I have to wear those high boots again? I still have a blister from yesterday."

"Yep. Those tennis shoes would stick out like a neon sign. We'll put a Band-Aid on your heel."

Rosemary Rita tried on some boots, and when she found the right ones, they paid the saleslady. Then they left for their final stop.

Mimi drove to Belk's Department Store. In the handbags section, she picked through the purses, bags, and backpacks. "I want to find just the right bag for you to carry. It has to be big enough to hold the hourglass and not so modern that it will stand out."

Stand-Outs:

Find the modern mistakes in old-fashioned pictures at winslowpress.com

"This cool purple backpack is out of the question, then?"

"Absolutely!"

"Oh, Mimi, look at this one," said

Rosemary Rita, holding up a green velvet drawstring bag.

"Sweetie, that's perfect."

"Really? Wow! I love it."

Mimi paid for the bag, and they left the store.

"Time to send you to Paris!" said Mimi. "Let's hurry home."

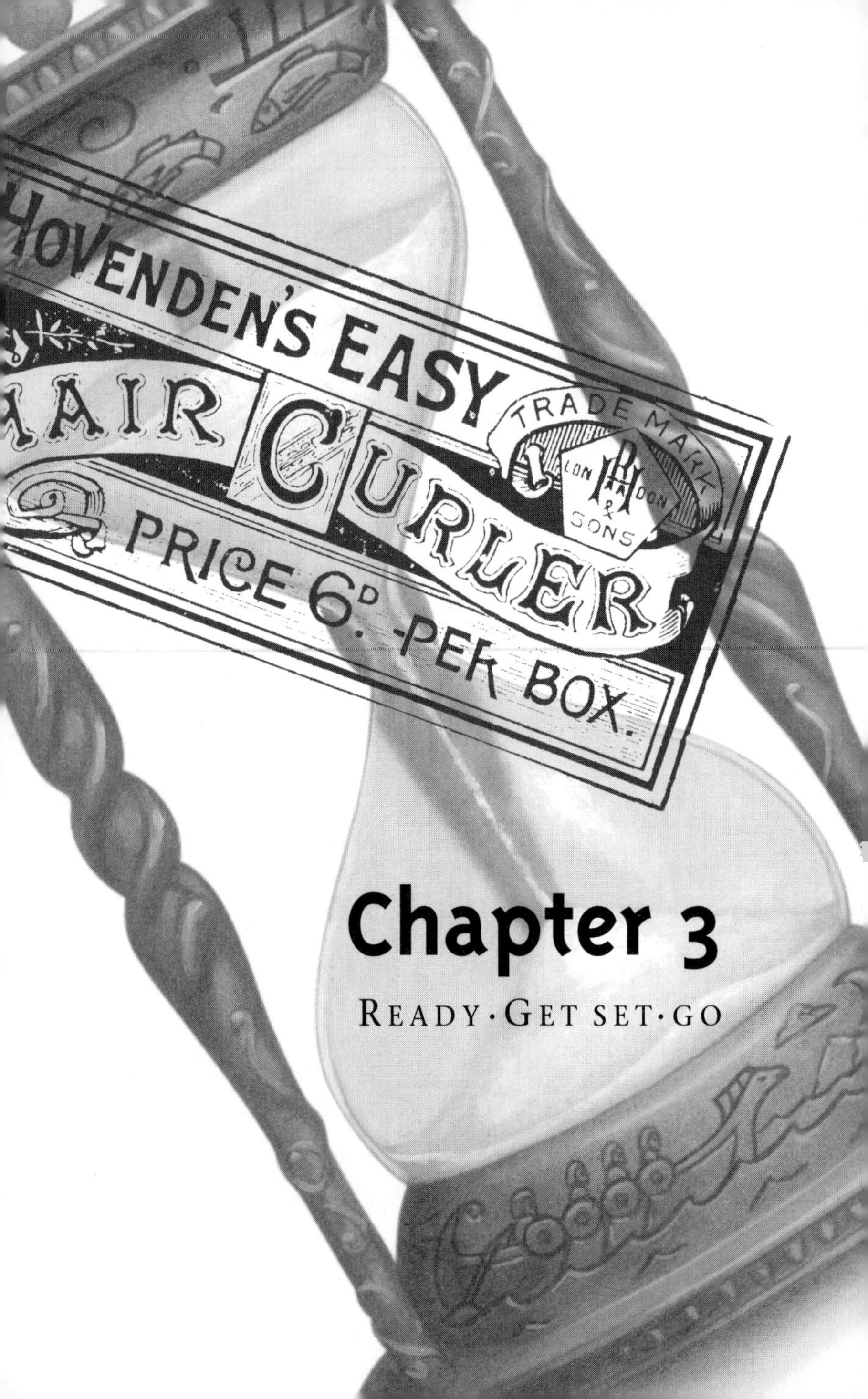

Chapter 3

Ready · Get set · go

HOVENDEN'S EASY
HAIR CURLER
TRADE MARK
R. HOVENDEN & SONS LONDON
PRICE 6D. PER BOX.

MIMI PULLED THE CAR INTO the driveway. They lifted the shopping bags from the backseat and went inside. On the kitchen counter was a note:

> Mom and Rosemary Rita,
>
> Ryan and I have gone to McDonald's. Help yourself to whatever you like in the fridge.
>
> Hope you two are having an exciting day.
>
> Love,
>
> Leigh

"How convenient!" said Mimi. "We can send you to Paris sooner than I thought."

"Great," said Rosemary Rita. "Can you help me change?"

Mimi nodded yes. Rosemary Rita let out a squeal of delight as she raced ahead to her room. She tore open the shopping bags and flung the dress and jacket on the bed. In a minute, her white shirt, purple sweater, and jeans were in a heap on the floor, and she had slipped on the green plaid dress. Mimi came through the door just in time to help fasten what seemed like a hundred buttons. Rosemary Rita put on the velvet jacket, and Mimi tied the sash around her waist. With the Band-Aid on her heel, the boots didn't hurt too much. Rosemary Rita paused to look at herself in the mirror.

"Hey, not bad. But something's not quite right. What do you think it is?"

"Your hair," said Mimi. "We need to curl it for a softer, more old-fashioned look. My curling iron should do the trick."

Soon Rosemary's Rita straight brown hair had been changed into a pile of soft ringlets.

"Now for the hat," said Rosemary Rita,

placing the green velvet hat on her head.

"That's it! You really do look like you stepped out of 1889!" exclaimed Mimi.

Hair-Raising:

Create new hairstyles for Rosemary Rita at winslowpress.com

"Okay. I'm ready now. Where's the postcard?"

"Not so fast, sweetie. I want you to study this map of the Exposition with me," said Mimi. "I found it last night on the Internet." Rosemary Rita huddled next to Mimi, gazing at the colorful map. Mimi pointed to the Eiffel Tower. "This is where Gracie is meeting Sophie. You'll recognize it, I'm sure. Now, you must promise to stay on the grounds of the fair, and not talk to any suspicious-looking strangers."

"I promise."

"And when it starts to get dark, I want you to flip the hourglass over and come home."

"Okay."

"Or, if you feel you are in danger, come home sooner."

"I'll be fine, Mimi. Don't worry."

"Well, I'm afraid I will worry, but I trust you. Just remember, you can turn the hourglass over if there's even a hint of trouble."

Site Seeing:

Visit the virtual exhibition with Rosemary's map at winslowpress.com

"Thanks, Mimi. I'll be careful, I promise."

"I know you will, dear, or I wouldn't let you go. Now let's get your little bag ready."

Mimi removed the tissue paper that covered the velvet drawstring bag. Then she reached into her own purse and pulled out a small tape recorder. "I thought you could take this along, too. This way, you can describe what you see while you're there. I want to hear every detail."

"Cool!" exclaimed Rosemary Rita.

"All right, we're ready. Here's the postcard," said Mimi, as she handed her granddaughter the old postcard from Paris.

Rosemary Rita took it and hugged her grandmother. "Be back in an hour.

See you then." She picked up the hourglass from her desk and sat on her bed. Her heart was pounding like a hammer hitting a nail. She took a deep breath and slowly exhaled.

While holding the postcard in one hand, she flipped over the hour-glass, then placed it in the velvet bag.

As the sand in the glass started to drip down to the bottom, she felt funny, kind of light in the head. Her stomach felt queasy, as if she'd just stepped off a roller-coaster ride. Suddenly, everything became blurry. She fell back into the pil-lows. Before she knew it, she had fallen into a deep, deep sleep.

Chapter 4

Paris · In · 1889

ROSEMARY RITA OPENED HER eyes and slowly looked around. She was still groggy from being asleep. The first thing she spotted was a cowboy wielding a lasso. He wore a brown suede vest with fringe at the bottom. A girl in a similar outfit twirled two guns in her hands as she stood on the dirt road in front of a saloon. Horses were hitched to the posts, and a crowd of people was gathered around.

"Oh, no! I've landed

in the wrong place. This can't be Paris. What should I do?" Rosemary Rita decided to ask someone. In her last adventure, she was able to understand and speak German. She hoped she would be speaking the language of wherever she was now.

Message Machine:

Send e-mails in different languages at winslowpress.com

Rosemary Rita saw a lady dressed in a full-length silk gown with a bustle on the back. "Excuse me, madam, but can you tell me where we are?"

"Can't you see? We are in the Wild West. That's Buffalo Bill and Annie Oakley over there," replied the lady, pointing.

Rosemary Rita groaned. "How could I have goofed? Now I'll never get to see Gracie and Paris. This stinks. I'll have to go back home and try again," she thought to herself.

As she reached inside her purse to get the hourglass, a big man with a handlebar moustache and a top hat bumped into her.

"Oh, *excusez-moi!* Excuse me!" he said.

"It's hard to watch where you're going with this great exhibit in progress."

"Exhibit? Yes, yes, of course," Rosemary Rita exclaimed. Then it dawned on her. "This must be one of the exhibits at the Exposition," she decided. "So I really am at the right place! I'd better hurry. I've got to get to the Eiffel Tower by ten o'clock, when Gracie and Sophie meet."

Oo la la!:

Everything about the Eiffel Tower at winslowpress.com

Rosemary Rita weaved through the colorfully dressed spectators, making her way to the exit. The men in their fancy coats and top hats tapped the ground with their canes. The women glided along beside them, their long, rustling skirts sweeping the path behind them. Rosemary Rita ducked through the tent flaps and blinked as she stepped outside into the sunlight. The reflection from the shiny copper-and-white marble almost blinded her. Rubbing her eyes, she gazed up at the ornate moldings and details on the buildings. Every inch of stone was decorated with statues, wrought-iron railings, and columns. Old-fashioned streetlights lined the wide, paved pathways. Electricity must have just been invented!

Rosemary Rita stepped onto the path behind an elegantly dressed couple. She was surprised to spot a fancy lace umbrella in the lady's gloved hand.

Sun Sets:

Play the parasol memory-match game at winslowpress.com

Rosemary Rita chuckled. "There isn't a cloud in the sky. What on earth is she doing with an umbrella?"

She glanced at her watch and realized that Gracie and Sophie would be meeting in less than ten minutes. Quickening her pace, she skipped through a maze of gardens. The beautiful colors of the flowers—red, yellow, pink, violet—were a blur as she hurried along. Finally she stood beneath the gleaming iron of the Eiffel Tower. It was enormous!

Rosemary Rita craned her neck and looked up. "Wow! It's so big and shiny. And it's red! The Eiffel Tower—I'm really here," thought Rosemary Rita. She checked her drawstring bag. The hourglass and tape recorder were still there.

Reaching around inside, she felt something else. "Hey, what's this?" She pulled out a pack of crackers, Skittles, and a Gatorade juice box. "Cool. Mimi made sure I wouldn't get hungry." Rosemary Rita picked up the tiny tape recorder and hid behind a large potted plant.

"Testing . . . 1, 2, 3. Okay, here goes. Paris is

incredible! Better than I dreamed it would be. I love to watch the people. They're all decked out. Most of the men are wearing top hats or straw hats and carrying walking sticks. The ladies are wearing beautiful long dresses, hats, and white gloves. And they have bustles, these huge bulges in the back of their dresses. What a difference from the tight skirts we wear. And the ladies' hats are hysterical. They are so big and frilly. I don't know how they walk around without falling on their faces. One of the hats looks like a nest. It even has a stuffed bird perched on top of it!

"I'm looking for Gracie and Sophie. I'm standing right in front of the Eiffel Tower. It's awesome—much better than in the pictures!

Hat Tricks:

Design your own hilarious headgear at winslowpress.com

There are small lakes at the bottom of it. This whole place is right out of a storybook. There are flowers everywhere. The buildings are so fancy, and they gleam in the sunlight. I can't believe they tore all this down when the fair was over. What a waste. Oh, Mimi, I see the bronze dome that you were talking about. That must be the Palace of Fine Arts. Wait, I think I see Gracie. There is a girl with blond hair, and wow—she looks just like Great-Great-Great-Grandmother Rosemarie. I can't see if she's wearing the...oh, she is!! She's wearing the locket, only it's not broken. All of it is there. But that's definitely her! I've got to go. I'm putting the recorder away for a while."

Chapter 5

The · Thief

ROSEMARY RITA STARED AT the ten-year-old girl who was only a few yards away. "There she is—my great-great-grandmother. This is too cool." Just then, another girl approached. She had brown ringlets and was wearing a lavender dress trimmed with lace. The girl slowed as she spotted Gracie, then hurried over to her.

Rosemary Rita held her breath. She wanted to run to the girls, but decided she'd better wait for the right time. The girls hugged one another and started talking at the same time.

"What a beautiful dress," squealed Gracie.

"*Merci beaucoup*. Thank you," said Sophie. "Maman had it made especially for this fair."

Parlez-Vous Français?

Check out the French audio phrase book at winslowpress.com

Rosemary Rita thought that Gracie's dress was even more beautiful than Sophie's. It was an unusual color of green that perfectly matched her eyes. Black velvet ribbon circled the collar, buttons, and skirt. She wore a pair of shoes with ribbons that tied around her ankles.

All of a sudden, a boy about their age dressed in dirty, torn clothes came running toward them. He came up close to Gracie and ripped the locket from her neck. Then he took off, zigzagging through the crowds.

The girls started screaming. "*Au secours!* Help! Someone, please, help!!!"

Without even thinking, Rosemary Rita dropped her bag, hiked up her skirt, and raced after the boy.

"I wish I wasn't wearing these stupid

boots," she panted.

Her hat went flying off and her curls flapped in the breeze. She was a fast runner, and the boy wasn't expecting a chase. Darting through the crowds and around the shrubbery, she caught up with the thief.

She dove forward and tackled the boy around the ankles. He was wearing black boots, and his blond hair was matted. His jacket was missing some buttons and his pants were grimy. They both went flying into the grassy area next to the path. The boy kicked and waved his arms, but Rosemary Rita was bigger. She pinned him to the ground with one knee. Then she grabbed the locket from his hand. He held tight. The locket broke in two. The boy lunged, and she fell to the side as he took off running. He got away with part of the locket, but she had saved most of it.

Lost Locket:

Can you solve the mystery of the missing locket at winslowpress.com?

Rosemary Rita pushed herself to her feet. She smoothed her hair and looked down at her dress. Other than a few grass stains, the dress seemed to have survived. Glancing up, she thought she saw the thief ducking into the last exhibit at the end of the path. She wanted to chase after him, but she also wanted to find Gracie and Sophie.

She turned and walked briskly back to the Eiffel Tower. Along the way, she found her hat and bag and picked them up. The girls were still standing where she had left them. They stared at Rosemary Rita with wide eyes and open mouths.

Gracie spoke first. "You were so brave to chase after that thief. He could have hurt you."

"It was nothing. I'm fine. Here's the part of the locket that I was able to get back," said Rosemary Rita as she placed it in Gracie's hand. "He got away as I grabbed it. I think we should go look for him. We might be able to get the rest of the locket back."

"You must be joking. We certainly can't chase him. It's much too dangerous," said Sophie.

"It's only dangerous if he sees us following him. What if the boy decided to throw away his piece of the locket because it's broken? Wouldn't you be happy to find it? Also, if we see him, we can get a better description of him for the police," said Rosemary Rita.

Goodness Gracie!:

Get to know Gracie at winslowpress.com

"You have to admit, Sophie, it does sound very exciting. We would be spies trying to solve the mystery of the missing locket," said Gracie.

"Oh, no, not you, too. First this strange girl and now you. If we follow that boy, we're sure to get in trouble."

"Well, I'd like to go," said

Gracie. "Come on, Sophie, don't be afraid. It will be fun. Let's go with..." Gracie paused and looked at Rosemary Rita. "We don't even know your name," she said. "My name is Gracie Christianson, *comment vous appelez-vous?* What's yours?"

"I'm Rose Hampton. It's nice to meet you, Gracie."

Rosemary Rita smiled to herself. "Yesterday, in Berlin, I was Rita," she thought. "Today, in Paris, I'm Rose. I guess that leaves the name Mary for my next adventure."

Sophie cleared her throat. "I'm Sophie LeGrand."

"Well, it's nice to meet both of you. I'd love to stand around and chat, but if I'm going to catch up with this thief, I'd better get going," said Rosemary Rita. "When I find the missing piece of the locket, I'll turn it in to the police."

"Rose, wait! We're coming, too," yelled Gracie as she yanked Sophie by the arm.

"No, we're not!" said Sophie. But as Gracie pulled her toward Rosemary Rita, she stopped protesting. "Oh, all right," she said. "But we have to be careful. Maman would kill me if she knew what I was doing."

"Mine, too," agreed Gracie. "But she'll never know."

"I saw him running toward the last exhibit at the end of the path," said Rosemary Rita. "Hopefully, he stuck around there for a while."

"Come on, *allons-y!* Let's go!" said Gracie. The three girls set out to catch the thief.

Chapter 6

The Hunt

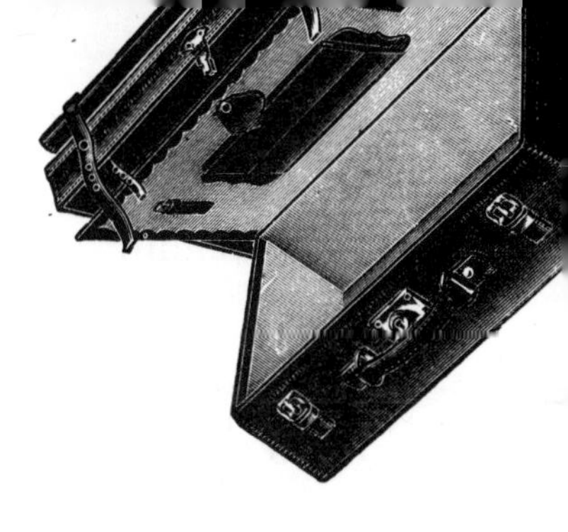

THEY WALKED BRISKLY along the neat paths of the Exposition. Passing the Palace of Fine Arts building, Rosemary Rita paused briefly to admire the carvings etched into the majestic dome. Below the dome, enormous arched windows were sandwiched between two towers with metal crowns.

They crossed in front of the French Gardens near the Palace of Machines. The girls stopped by the grassy area where Rosemary Rita had been pushed down. "Here's where we wrestled," said Rosemary

Rita, pointing to the place behind the bushes. "Let's look around and see if he dropped the other part of the locket."

Sophie moaned. "I can't spend too long here. I want to see the sights. Maman said that I could drop a balloon message from the Eiffel Tower. This is a waste of time."

"Oh, Sophie, don't you think this is exciting? Let's just look for a little while. If nothing turns up, we'll all go throw balloons from the Eiffel Tower." Gracie crouched in the grass, looking for a glimpse of the locket.

"I don't mean to spoil your fun," blurted Rosemary Rita. "I know that you two have waited a long time to meet each other."

"Wait a minute. How do you know that?" Sophie asked.

Rosemary Rita froze. "Oh, just something you said," she remarked quickly. "Let's start looking behind the bushes and in the flower beds," she added, hoping Sophie would be distracted from asking any more questions.

"All right," said Gracie. "Now where exactly were you when you grabbed the locket from him? Did you see him run into the exhibit at the end or just run toward it?"

"The spot I showed you over here is exactly where he pushed me down before running away. I thought I saw him enter the last exhibit, but I'm not really sure. I hope he's still on the fairgrounds," said Rosemary Rita.

The girls searched in the grass and shrubbery, but nothing turned up. They decided to walk in the direction in which the thief had been last seen. Unfortunately, they did not spot the missing part of the locket on the path, either. They finally arrived at the exhibit at the end—the Egyptian Bazaar.

People were bustling around everywhere. Waiters, vendors, and craftsmen, dressed in colorful costumes, flooded the streets. One man wore a hat shaped like a small box, with a tassel on the end. His baggy purple pants blew in the wind. The tips of his satin shoes rolled up in a curl.

At least twenty shops and restaurants were crowded together. The smell of exotic Egyptian foods filled the air. Rosemary Rita's

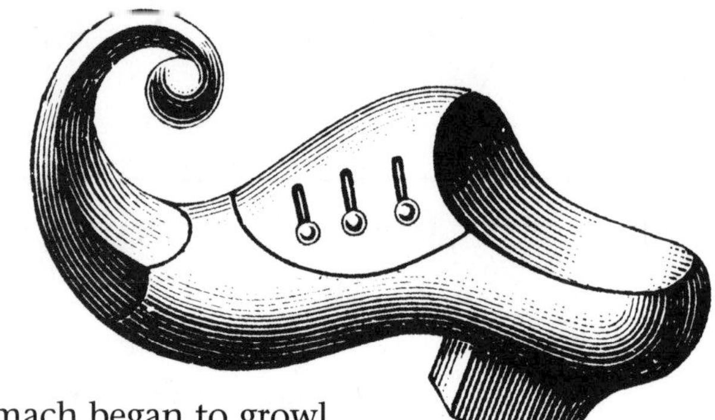

stomach began to growl.

"Let's eat something while we're here," suggested Sophie. "Look at all those honey pastries!"

"It is almost lunchtime," said Gracie. "I'm starting to get hungry."

"We don't have time," said Rosemary Rita. "I'm hungry, too, but we can't stop. We have to keep moving if we're going to catch that thief."

"We'll never catch him," said Sophie. "Besides, I didn't come to the biggest fair in the world to be a spy. I want to enjoy myself."

Rosemary Rita's stomach growled again.

"You win," she said finally. They went over to a stand and bought some fata, a lamb and bread stew. For dessert, they had pastries and cinnamon tea.

A crowd had gathered in front of one of the restaurants. "Let's see what's going on," said Gracie. The girls nudged their way through the crowd.

"Oh, my, look at those ladies! I've never seen anyone dance like that!" exclaimed Sophie.

"I've never even seen anyone dressed like that," added Gracie.

Mix Master:

Create your own tunes with sounds from around the world at winslowpress.com

The girls watched the belly dancers move in their billowing scarves. The dancers swayed their hips from side to side, twisting their bodies to the rhythm of the music. A very fat man with dark skin and a beard played a tune on his flute. Rosemary Rita excused herself for a minute and stepped behind a column. She pulled out her tape recorder. After she made sure that no one was watching, she turned it on and said, "Mimi, you'll never believe what I'm watching—belly dancers! The ladies are wearing veils over their faces, sheer skirts, and jewels in their belly buttons!"

Fabulous Foods:

Sample a smorgasbord of international foods at winslowpress.com

Rosemary Rita clicked off the recorder and tossed it back in her bag. She munched a few Skittles, then returned to the girls. The belly dancers had stopped. "Let's go into one of the shops," said Sophie. "I'd like to buy a scarf for a souvenir."

Suddenly Gracie let out a gasp and said, "Look! There's the thief."

"Stay calm!" cautioned Rosemary Rita. "He hasn't spotted us yet. Let's quietly follow behind him."

"Maybe we should hide in that archway and watch where he goes," said Sophie.

The girls ducked beneath the arch and watched as the boy turned and headed toward them. Luckily, he went into a fenced-in area behind one of the restaurants. Two more boys followed him into the same area. They too had on filthy, tattered clothes. One boy was barefoot, and a big scar ran across his left cheek. The other boy was carrying an old, battered suitcase.

"Something is definitely going on behind that fence," said Rosemary Rita.

"Let's see if there's a hole or something we can peek through," whispered Gracie.

"I think we should forget the whole thing," said Sophie. " I don't like the look of those boys."

"We can't quit now," said Rosemary Rita. "Not when we're this close to finding something out."

Sophie shook her head. Her eyebrows formed a worried frown. "I don't want to go."

"You have to!" said Gracie.

"Well, I'll go if you promise we'll stay on this side of the fence," said Sophie. "I guess there's no harm in just looking at them."

"Of course there's not," said Rosemary Rita. "Come on." The girls crept along the fence. Finally they found a broken spot in the wooden pickets. They looked through the small opening. Twelve boys were huddled together. Scattered around them were silver and gold pieces, jewels, bags, papers, books, watches, and other valuables. Some of the stuff was spilling out of the leather suitcase one of the boys had been carrying.

"A den of thieves!" cried Gracie.

"Shh! They'll hear you," whispered Rosemary Rita.

Up to No Good:

Check out creepy criminals of the late 1800s at winslowpress.com

"This is horrible. We need to go to the police," said Sophie.

As Rosemary Rita leaned forward to get a better view, she accidentally stepped on Gracie's foot.

Gracie let out a loud yelp.

"What was that?" said the boy with the scar, looking around.

Rosemary Rita's heart began

racing. She held her breath. The other girls crouched with their hands over their mouths.

"It's probably nothing, just one of those alley cats," said a boy wearing a blue cap.

"We'd better move out, just in case," said the thief who had taken the locket. "Let's meet back here in an hour."

The boys jumped up. They gathered their stuff and shoved it into the suitcase. Then they ran through a gap on the other side of the fence. Within minutes they were gone.

"I'm sorry," said Gracie. "I guess I scared them away."

"It's not your fault. I'm sorry I stepped on your foot," said Rosemary Rita.

"What should we do now?" asked Gracie.

"I'm not sure. We can't catch all twelve of them. Let's take a look at what they left behind." Rosemary Rita pointed toward the other side of the fence. "One of them dropped something."

"I don't know, Rose. It seems risky." Sophie was twisting the fabric of her skirt between her fingers.

"You heard what they said. They won't be back for an hour. We've scared them away. Besides, aren't you curious?"

"It's probably garbage," said Sophie.

"Well, I think it must be something important, or they wouldn't have stolen it in the first place," said Rosemary Rita. Before Sophie or Gracie could argue, she circled the fence and darted through the gap. Picking up the forgotten item, she ran back to the girls.

Chapter 7

Lost · And · Found

ROSEMARY RITA WAS HOLDING A white scroll tied with a black string. She started to undo it.

Sophie grabbed Rosemary Rita's arm. "Wait! This is too much. First, you have us chasing all over the Exposition after a thief, then you take a stolen item. I don't like this one bit, and I won't be a part of it. Come on, Gracie, let's go."

"I, uh, I'm sorry, Sophie, but I want to stay," stammered Gracie.

"What do you mean, you want to stay? You don't even know this girl. She has placed us in danger. What if the thieves come back?"

"I don't think we're in danger, and I'm curious!" said Gracie.

"Fine. You two deserve each other. I'm leaving," said Sophie. She marched off toward the path.

"If you want to go after her, I understand," said Rosemary Rita.

"Thank you, but she needs to calm down a bit. I'll catch up with her later, but right now, I want to see what's on the scroll."

"I'm curious, too," said Rosemary Rita, unrolling it. It was an oil painting of a lovely young blond girl in a bonnet. She was sitting on a hill with flowers in her hand. The artist had signed *E. Potthast* at the bottom of the canvas.

"Oh, *magnifique!* It's beautiful!" exclaimed Gracie.

"It really is wonderful. I've always liked this kind of painting."

"Me, too. I like the soft lines. What do we do now?" asked Gracie.

"I guess we'd better try to find the artist who painted it. He's probably at the Exposition," replied Rosemary Rita as she rolled up the canvas and retied it.

"Let's go to the Palace of Fine Arts building. Most of the artists are exhibiting there," said Gracie.

"Okay. I know exactly where it is. We passed it on our way here," said Rosemary Rita.

The girls walked by a small lake with fountains spouting water. In no time, they had arrived at the Palace of Fine Arts. Together they climbed the steps and hurried inside.

The first thing they noticed were all of the statues scattered throughout the enormous room. The ceiling soared above them, and a balcony circled the room with artwork displayed on the walls behind it. Two U-shaped staircases led to the upper floor.

"This is so amazing!" said Rosemary Rita.

"Let's go up to the balcony," said Gracie. The girls held onto the ornate iron railings as they climbed more steps.

"What next?" asked Gracie.

"Let's ask someone if they know where we can find *Monsieur* Potthast," suggested Rosemary Rita.

The girls walked along the balcony, admiring the beautiful paintings hanging on the walls. Gracie spotted a gentleman wearing a badge.

"Excuse me, *monsieur.* We are looking for an artist named E. Potthast. We believe he is exhibiting here," said Gracie.

The man smiled. "Yes, he is. *Je m'appelle* William Chase. My

name is William Chase, and I'm an artist, too. We're both exhibiting in the American section. Would you like me to take you there?"

"Oh, thank you," cooed Gracie. "My name is Gracie Christianson and this is my friend Rose Hampton."

"I'm delighted to meet you both," replied Mr. Chase, as he led them through a door to the galleries of American paintings.

"There are so many paintings!" exclaimed Rosemary Rita.

"Yes, we have the largest display, after France, of course. We are showing three hundred thirty-six paintings by one hundred eighty-nine different artists. In fact, we had so many paintings, we had to hang some over the windows to make room," stated Mr. Chase.

"If you don't mind, sir, could we see your paintings first?" asked Gracie.

"I was hoping you would ask," he laughed. "Here they are—these eight are mine." There were three large portraits, a city park scene, and several landscapes.

"I like this one. It reminds me of Central Park," said Rosemary Rita, pointing to *A City Park*.

"Why, you are absolutely right. It is Central Park. Such a young girl, and you've already traveled to America!" exclaimed Mr. Chase.

Rosemary Rita blushed. "I, uh, have family in New York. I recognized it from a postcard," she said, trying not to sound nervous.

"Truly remarkable," mumbled Mr. Chase. "Now I'll show you Edward Potthast's painting. It's in the gallery over here."

"We'd love to see his painting," said Gracie. "But we really were looking for him."

"Oh, dear. Well, he's not here now—"

"Oh, no. We have to find him. It's urgent," said Rosemary Rita.

"I was about to say that he's not here now, but he should be back in about fifteen minutes. Perhaps you'd like to wait for him?"

"Yes, please. Thank you so much for your help, Mr. Chase," said Rosemary Rita.

"It was very nice to meet you," added Gracie.

"The pleasure was all mine. It was a welcome break from all of these fussy artists," said Mr. Chase, as he waved good-bye.

The girls sat down on one of the large, round velvet sofas in the middle of the room.

"Let's look around while we're waiting," said Rosemary Rita.

"All right," said Gracie. "The American paintings look really interesting."

Masterpiece Maze:

Can you find your way through the gallery at winslowpress.com?

The two girls gazed at portraits of high-society ladies and of peasant girls. They saw pictures of angels and of children. Landscapes showed everything from sandy beaches to mountain scenes to fields dotted with flowers. While some paintings looked more than ten feet tall, others looked only about a foot wide.

On one wall, Rosemary Rita counted as many as thirty-three paintings. As she moved toward the next gallery, she noticed a door marked *Femmes*. It had a silhouette of a lady in a long dress painted on the door. "That must be the ladies' room," she thought to herself. "I'll be right back," she said to Gracie. "I need to go to the bathroom."

It was an old-fashioned bathroom with beautiful, large oval mirrors on the wall. The shiny white sinks had lovely brass faucets, and the toilet bowls were separated by curtains, with chains for flushing. Rosemary Rita stood by the wall, switched on the tape recorder, and started naming the artists: "Kenyon Cox, Alfred Bricher, E. L. Henry, John Singer Sargent...Mimi, there are so many artists' paintings here. I know that I'll never remember all of their names. This tape recorder is a great idea."

She turned off the recorder and went back to join Gracie.

"While you were in the ladies' room," said Gracie, "I found Mr. Potthast's painting. Come on, I'll show you. It's called *A Young Brittany Girl.*"

Rosemary Rita followed her to the painting. "Look, Gracie, it's just like the one that we found! It is beautiful. Look at how bright the colors are and how sweet the girl looks."

A voice from behind said, "That is nice praise coming from one so young."

The girls whirled around to face the artist they had been searching for, Edward Potthast.

Chapter 8

The · Artist

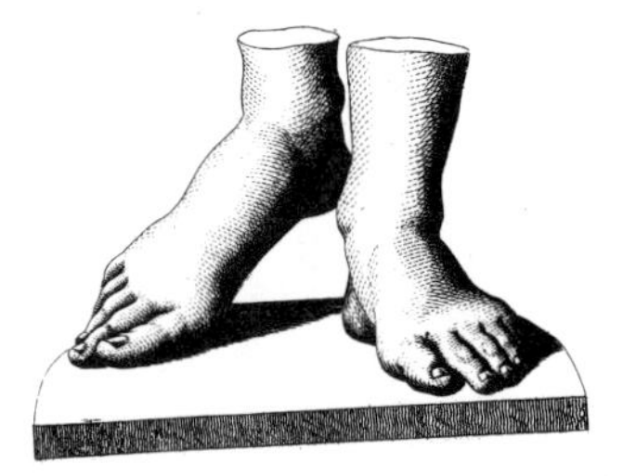

THEY STARED UP AT A TALL man wearing a loose-fitting black shirt and a beret. A little red scarf was tied around his neck.

"Why, you're not that old!" blurted Rosemary Rita.

"Rose!" exclaimed Gracie.

He smiled. "Thank you."

"Excuse me. I expected you to be older because you're exhibiting at such an important event," explained Rosemary Rita.

"*Ça va.* That's all right. I understood what you meant. Actually, I am thirty-two years old. Not exactly old, but certainly not young anymore."

"You're just a little bit younger than my mom. Do you have any children? Is this your daughter in the painting?" asked Rosemary Rita.

"No, I don't have any children of my own, but I do have nieces and nephews that I sketch. Now, Mr. Chase told me that you girls were looking for me. What can I do for you?"

"Please excuse our bad manners," said Gracie. "I'm Gracie Christianson and this is my friend Rose Hampton."

"We were trying to find you because we have something of yours we think was stolen," Rosemary Rita explained. She handed Mr. Potthast the canvas.

He let out a gasp. "It is mine. Where did you girls get this?"

"It's a long story, but a young boy stole my locket. . . ." said Gracie.

"I chased after him and was able to get part of it back, but he got away," interrupted Rosemary Rita.

"*Mon Dieu.* My goodness. That sounds dangerous. Young girls chasing after thieves."

"That's what my friend Sophie thought," said Gracie.

"Who's Sophie?" asked Mr. Potthast.

"She's a girl that I was exchanging post-cards with. We met today at the fair. She didn't like us getting involved with stolen goods, so she stormed off."

"Well, I must say that as grateful as I am to have this back, I agree with your friend Sophie. Have you told the authorities about this thief?" asked Mr. Potthast.

"There wasn't just one thief, there were twelve," stated Gracie.

"Twelve! Now that really is dangerous. But I still don't understand what your stolen locket has to do with my stolen painting."

Rosemary Rita and Gracie explained the events of the past two hours.

"We came to find you so that we could return your painting," Rosemary Rita finished. "It's so much like the one you're exhibiting here."

"It's a study," said Mr. Potthast. "I painted it before the final picture you just looked at. Do you want to see some other sketches I've been working on?" he asked.

Art Class:

Ever wonder how artists do it? See a painting made step by step at winslowpress.com

"Oh, yes!" the girls chimed.

He opened the large satchel he was carrying and pulled out a sketchbook. There was a sketch of the Eiffel Tower, and another of the Palace of Machines. There was an unfinished one of the back of a little girl looking up at the Eiffel Tower.

Gracie spoke first. "I think you're very talented. Would you like to sketch me?"

"Gracie, you can't ask him to do that," said Rosemary Rita.

"It's all right. I'd be happy to," he said. He turned a page in his book and pulled out a pencil.

Picture-Perfect:

Create masterpieces with the magic paintbrush at winslowpress.com

Gracie stood very still as his pencil made scratching noises on the paper. In a few minutes, he had drawn a quick likeness of her.

"Here, what do you think?"

"It looks just like her!" declared Rosemary Rita.

"Would you like to keep it?" asked Mr. Potthast, ripping the paper from his book.

"No, you keep it," said Gracie. "Maybe I'll get lucky and turn up in one of your paintings someday!"

They all laughed.

"I'd better be getting back to work," said Mr. Potthast. "Thank you so much for finding my lost painting. You are very brave girls."

"It was nice to meet you," said Rosemary Rita.

"I enjoyed it, too. And one more thing. Try to find your friend Sophie. She was right, you know. You're lucky that you weren't hurt."

Rosemary Rita grimaced. She could do without Sophie's complaints for a while longer.

"Time to go," she said, taking Gracie's arm. "We still need to find the missing piece of your locket."

The girls skipped down the grand staircase and out the door.

Chapter 9

The · Capture

As they walked down the stone steps to the path, they heard chimes coming from the bell tower.

"Oh no, it's three o'clock!" exclaimed Rosemary Rita.

"What's the matter?" asked Gracie.

"We only have about twenty minutes until the boys meet up again behind the fence. We've got to go to the police," she said.

They turned the corner and went down another path. Right next to a large glass case displaying elegant ladies' clothing was a security booth. A small elderly woman sat reading inside. She had tiny eyes that almost disappeared behind the lenses of her glasses.

"Excuse me, Madam," panted Rosemary Rita. "We need to speak to a police officer right away."

The woman put down her book, removed her glasses, and slowly rubbed her chin. "Nobody here but me," she said, picking up her book again.

"Wait," cried Gracie. "We need some help."

The woman sighed. "Sorry, dears, you'll have to come back later."

"Later! We can't come back. . . ." Gracie said.

"It's no use," said Rosemary Rita, as she pulled her away from the booth. "We'll have to capture the thieves ourselves."

"Just the two of us, are you kidding?" asked Gracie. "Two girls against twelve boys? You're crazy!"

"What we lack in numbers and strength,

we'll make up for with brainpower," said Rosemary Rita.

"Brainpower?" said Gracie.

"Yes, brainpower," said Rosemary Rita, pointing to her head. "We'll put our minds together and outsmart them. Come on, let's hurry."

"Where are we going?" asked Gracie.

"Back to the Egyptian Exhibit," said Rosemary Rita.

"Oh no, not me," said Gracie, pulling away.

"Don't worry," said Rosemary Rita. "I've got a plan."

"That's what I was afraid of," said Gracie, letting out a nervous laugh.

"I promise, I won't put us in danger. Now, let's go. We're running out of time."

The girls hiked up their skirts and hurried through the fair. They muttered apologies as they nearly plowed down a family of four. Within minutes, they were back inside the Egyptian Exhibit. There was a huge crowd gathered outside the fenced-in area. A large number of police were there, swarming around the thieves. The thieves were yelling and screaming. The crowd was cheering the police.

"The police are already here," said Gracie. "How did they know?"

The girls looked at each other, then said at the same time, "Sophie!"

Sure enough, off to the side of the crowd stood Sophie. Gracie and Rosemary Rita ran over to her.

"Sophie, you're here!" said Gracie.

"Well, I decided someone needed to do something. I wasn't going to spend my whole time chasing after a bunch of dirty boys, but I certainly didn't want them to get away, either," said Sophie.

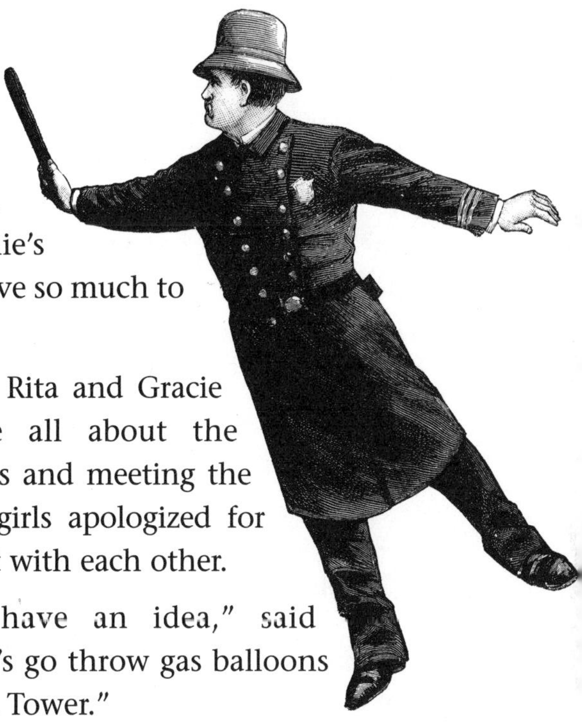

"You did a great job," said Gracie, taking Sophie's arm. "We have so much to tell you."

Rosemary Rita and Gracie told Sophie all about the stolen canvas and meeting the artists. The girls apologized for getting upset with each other.

"Hey, I have an idea," said Sophie. "Let's go throw gas balloons off the Eiffel Tower."

Message from Above:

Catch the balloons to solve silly riddles at winslowpress.com

"That will be a nice change after those thieves," said Rosemary Rita. "Excuse me for just a minute." She ducked into the bathroom and reached into her bag for the tape recorder. As she felt around the inside of the bag, she noticed that something was missing. She dumped everything out of her purse onto the sink.

"Oh, no!" she exclaimed as she examined the contents. "The hourglass is gone! Where can it be?" She tried to remember the last time she'd had it. "I know that it was here when I first used the recorder. But then what? Oh my gosh, what if it fell out when I was chasing that boy?" Rosemary Rita took several deep breaths. Her heart was beating in her throat.

"I've got to calm down," she said, breathing deeply and blowing some air out of her mouth. "The hourglass must be somewhere. I have to find it or I'll be stuck here forever!"

She shoved everything back into her bag and hurried out of the bathroom. She whizzed by Gracie and Sophie.

"Rose! Where are you going?" Gracie called after her.

"Huh? Oh, I, uh, need to get home. Throw a balloon off the tower for me."

"Wait, you can't go now. Not when we're going to have some fun."

"Come with us, Rose," urged Sophie, though her voice was flat.

Gracie rolled her eyes. "That didn't sound very convincing."

"It's going to be wonderful," said Sophie, as Gracie poked her with her elbow. "We'll be able to see the whole fair from the top of the Eiffel Tower."

"I'd really like to go," said Rosemary Rita. "But I can't. I completely forgot that I was supposed to meet my grandmother at three o'clock. I'm already very late."

"Then you'd better get going. Your grandmother's probably getting worried about you. Thanks for all of your help. I'm so glad we met," said Gracie.

"Me, too," added Sophie.

"Thanks," Rosemary Rita said, hugging the girls. "I'll never forget this day. Good-bye."

She hurried out of the Egyptian Exhibit and trotted down the path leading to the Eiffel Tower. She walked as if she had blinders on. She didn't pause to admire the manicured bushes that lined the paths. She didn't notice the elegantly dressed people milling around the fountain. In fact, she was so focused on finding the hourglass that she didn't see the stone bench directly in front of her! She tripped over it and went flying into the grass.

"Ouch!" she exclaimed, scrambling to her feet. Her dress was crumpled and stained. Her hair was a tangled mess. A tear rolled down her cheek. She quickly wiped it away. "I can't get upset. I have to stay calm. I need to get to where I threw down my bag when I was chasing that thief!"

Rosemary Rita smoothed her skirt, took a deep breath, and continued on. In a few minutes, she arrived at the exact spot. She searched the area on her hands and knees. Nothing. Rosemary Rita's stomach was in knots. She had a lump the size of a grapefruit in her throat. "This can't be happening to me. What am I going to do? What would Mimi do?"

Right then, a small, red-headed girl ran by her. Sunlight flashed on the object the girl was holding. Rosemary Rita held her breath. "Could it be the hourglass? Please, let it be my hourglass," she prayed. "Yes, it *is* my hourglass!" she exclaimed as she got a better look.

A thin woman with a pointy nose and a navy uniform followed behind the girl. The woman raised one eyebrow and pursed her lips tightly together as she watched Rosemary Rita stare at the child. Rosemary Rita ignored the woman and darted ahead to catch up to the girl.

She moved slowly, trying not to frighten her. Forcing herself to speak in a relaxed, friendly manner, she said, "Hello. My name is Rose, what's yours?"

The girl didn't answer.

"What's that you're playing with? May I see it?" asked Rosemary Rita, as she gently held out her hand.

The girl looked up at Rosemary Rita. She stared back down at the hourglass. Then she pulled back her arm, as if ready to throw a football, and hurled the hourglass into the nearby lake!

"Oh no! What have you just done?!" screamed Rosemary Rita, running toward the water. Without a moment's thought, she dove in after the hourglass. The water made her dress and boots heavy, pulling her down and making it difficult to swim. Rosemary Rita frantically swished her arms, diving deeper and running her hands along the bottom to find the hourglass. As she popped up for a quick breath, she saw several men wading into the water. She quickly ducked back under to continue her search. Finally, her fingers touched something that felt like it might be, yes, it *was* the wooden stand! She grasped it just as something tugged at her feet. With all her might, she squirmed free. A moment later, three soggy

Frenchmen lifted her out of the water.

A crowd had gathered by the lake. The red-headed girl was bawling, and the people were pointing and yelling. The men who had grabbed Rosemary Rita were being cheered by the spectators.

One of the dripping men pointed toward Rosemary Rita. He declared, "*Voilà,* I have saved the girl."

"No, no, it was me. I am the one," insisted the tall man in the vest.

"*Excusez moi,* you are mistaken. I pulled her by the foot," said the third man with the firm grip.

The men moved closer to each other. They spoke faster and louder. They waved their arms wildly. The crowd leaned forward to hear better. Everyone was talking at once. In the confusion, Rosemary Rita quietly stepped onto shore. She jumped behind a bush and flipped the hourglass over.

As the sand in the glass started to drip to the bottom, she felt funny, kind of light in the head. Her stomach felt queasy, as if she'd just stepped off a roller-coaster ride. Suddenly, everything became blurry. Before she knew it, she had fallen into a deep, deep sleep.

Chapter 10

Home · Again

ROSEMARY RITA SAT UP AND opened her eyes. Everything was a little blurry. She felt around with her hands and discovered her little stuffed bear. "Little Browner, it's you, buddy. I'm home!" she said, picking him up. "Boy, that was close. I almost ended up in nineteenth-century Paris for the rest of my life!"

Her eyes adjusted, and she looked at the clock. Only an hour had passed.

"This is so cool. Just like last time. I've only been away for an hour of our time. I need to find Mimi and tell her all about it." She leapt out of bed.

The water in her boots spilled onto the rug. Her dress was so heavy with lake water that she could hardly move. "What a mess!" said Rosemary Rita, sloshing to the bathroom. Her hat felt like it weighed a ton. Water dripped off the brim as she pried it off her head. She unbuttoned the dress and slipped it off. She sat down on the edge of the bathtub and yanked off the boots, making puddles on the floor.

"Feels good to get those off," sighed Rosemary Rita, rubbing her feet.

Returning to her bedroom, she yanked on her tan jeans, white shirt, and purple sweater. She stood in front of the mirror and pulled her brush through her wet hair, trying to get the knots out. It was useless. Her beautiful ringlets were now a pile of soggy tangles. She gave up and pulled her hair back into a ponytail. Then she mopped up the puddles that the boots had made on the rug and floor.

"Time to visit with Mimi!" she exclaimed.

She ran down the stairs and burst into the guestroom. Her grandmother was curled up on her bed, reading a book.

"Mimi, Mimi! I'm back. It was wonderful," said Rosemary Rita, wrapping her arms around her grandmother.

"Oh, darling, you're here safe and sound. I'm so relieved. I've hardly been able to concentrate for the last hour because of worrying about you."

"A million exciting things happened to me. I can't wait to tell you all about it. I used the tape recorder you sent, too, but I'm afraid it got wet. First I landed at the Buffalo Bill and Annie Oakley exhibit. They were twirling guns and swinging lassos. I thought that I had gone back to the wrong place in time!"

"That's so funny. What happened next?"

Rosemary Rita described meeting the girls and chasing after the thief.

Mimi interrupted, "There was a thief?!"

"Don't worry, I was fine. I tackled him to get Gracie's locket back."

"You *what*?" asked Mimi in disbelief.

Rosemary Rita tripped over her words as she gushed out the whole story of her adventure. When she was finished, Mimi hugged her tightly.

"You are a very lucky young lady! You could've been trapped in 1889. My, what a lot of excitement! Hey, I just thought of something. A painting by Edward Potthast is hanging in this house. Isn't that amazing? What a coincidence! I gave the painting to your mom for her birthday a few years ago, and I think she hung it in her bedroom."

"I know which one you mean," cried Rosemary Rita, taking Mimi's hand. "Let's go see it!" Together, they scurried down the hall to her parents' room.

Rosemary Rita gazed at the painting on the wall. "I can't believe it. It's really his. He signed E. Potthast at the bottom, just like at the Exposition!" She gasped. "It's so neat—he painted this, and the girl looks just like Gracie!"

Mimi leaned forward and looked at the painting. "Do you really think it is Gracie?"

"I can't be sure, but it could be her. He did do that sketch of her. Maybe he used it for the face of the girl on the beach. Wouldn't that be so cool? Gracie would have been thrilled to see this. Where did you get this painting?"

"It was my mother's. She got it from her mother—which would mean Gracie gave it to her."

"Wow! Then it could have happened. It could really be Gracie! Mimi, this has been the most exciting spring break ever!"

"The good news is that it's not even over. But I'm afraid I have to go home tomorrow.

They need me at work."

"Oh, no. You can't leave yet. I want to go on another adventure."

"Sweetie, you need to take a little break from your adventures. You should go roller blading with your friends."

"I can't. My friends are all away. Besides, playing with them isn't nearly as exciting as going back in time."

"Let's go downstairs and fix a nice snack. We'll save our talk about hourglasses and postcards for later."

"All right," said Rosemary Rita reluctantly. She followed her grandmother to the kitchen.

Ryan and her mom had come back from McDonald's, and they were playing on the floor. Ryan was crawling around, barking like a dog.

Rosemary Rita got down on all fours and started barking back at him. Then she stopped.

"Ryan, where did you get that dog collar? Have you been in my room?" cried Rosemary Rita, as she tried to get the collar off her brother.

Ryan started to cry, "Mo-m-my!"

"Rosemary Rita, stop it," said her mother. "Be nice."

"Mom, that's mine," she said, pointing to the collar. "It was in one of my birthday boxes. He's been going through my stuff again."

Talk Back:

Tell Rosemary Rita about your annoying sibling at winslowpress.com

"Don't forget, he's only two. You know he didn't mean any harm."

"But how's he going to learn if you don't say something?" protested Rosemary Rita.

"Okay. Ryan, buddy, that collar belongs to Rosemary Rita. You have to give it back."

Ryan barked and scurried off into the playroom.

"Mom, *do* something!" shouted Rosemary Rita.

"Calm down. There's no need to yell."

"He drives me crazy! He's always messing with my things."

Just then, Mimi walked in from the

playroom. She handed the collar to Rosemary Rita. "This little puppy and I are going to go out for a walk," said Mimi, carrying Ryan to the back door.

"Wait, I'll come, too," said Mom. "Do you want to join us, Rosemary Rita?"

"No, thanks. I'm going to my room. I want to make sure Ryan didn't take anything else."

"Okay. See you in a little while."

Rosemary Rita walked up the stairs and down the hall. She flopped onto her four-poster bed and stared at the dog collar. There were three initials engraved on the front of the round pendant hanging from the collar—RSM.

"I wonder what these initials stand for?" Rosemary Rita picked up the stack of postcards. "I bet the answer is on one of these cards. . . . and who knows, maybe that's where my next adventure will take place."

The • End

EXPOSITION
1889
CHEZ
SOI
FLVCTVAT NEC MERGITVR
L'INDUSTRIE EST L'UNION DE L'ART ET DE LA SCIENCE

A Note from the Author

Stepping into the Past

In 1889, Paris invited the world to come and visit. The Exposition had displays of all that was new and exciting in business, the sciences, and the arts. Although France held an Exposition every eleven years between 1867 and 1900, the 1889 *Exposition Universelle* (Universal Exposition), where Rosemary Rita had her adventure, was by far the most successful. It marked the one hundredth anniversary of the fall of the Bastille, the beginning of the French Revolution.

In the hundred years since the revolution, France had gone through much turmoil. But by 1889, France's Third Republic had been stable for eighteen years. The country was growing wealthier and more democratic. France wanted to show other countries that it could lead. It wanted to show the world what it could do.

The Exposition

The Eiffel Tower was begun in January

1887 and completed early in 1889. It was built especially for the Exposition. It showed off the strength of French engineering, science, and art. Even today, it is a symbol of France that is recognized all over the world. But when it was first completed, many Parisians were outraged. They thought it was one of the ugliest things they had ever seen. A group was formed to protest its existence. Some of them called it a "metal asparagus," and said that it ruined the appearance of the city.

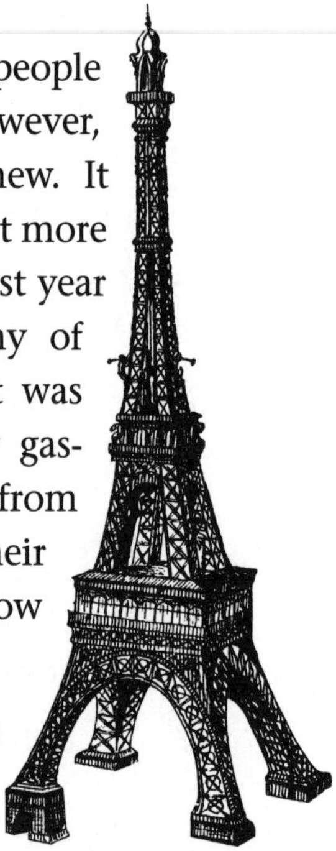

To most of the 32 million people who attended the Exposition, however, the Tower was exciting and new. It turned out to be so popular that it more than paid for itself during the first year of its existence. In 1889, many of Paris's young people thought it was fun to attach messages to tiny gas-filled balloons and drop them from the Tower's upper platform. Their friends waited on the ground below to catch them.

A different structure, the

Café
Restaurant
72

History of Habitation, also attracted attention. It included thirty-three buildings. Each one was built like a dwelling of the past, from caves to mansions. Another building, the Pavilion of the Ministry of War, was built to look like a castle from the Middle Ages. It had a drawbridge and was meant to represent military strength.

Paris was proud of its latest technological advancements, including electricity. It is said that 1889 was the year in which Paris became known as the "City of Lights." The entire Exposition grounds and buildings had electric lights. The Eiffel Tower, which was then the world's tallest tower, was covered in lights. Thomas Alva Edison, the inventor of the lightbulb, climbed the Tower and signed its guest book. And it wasn't just the Exposition grounds that were lit by the *fée électricité* ("fairy lights"). This was also the year when the first electric lighting went into many of Paris's public buildings, including theaters, stores, and train stations.

The huge fairgrounds, with their acres of exhibition halls, gardens, restaurants, and displays, covered a large part of central Paris. Celebrities and "distinguished visitors" came from all over the world to visit this huge event. Buffalo Bill Cody and his Wild West Show came from America to perform at the Exposition.

Dozens of countries were represented in the exhibits. The "Colonial" section was where France displayed examples of the cultures from the countries it controlled in Asia and Africa. In fact, some countries were "reproduced" at the Exposition. Visitors could stroll through a Cambodian village or watch Javanese dancers. As Rosemary Rita and her friends did, they could visit the "reconstitution" of an Egyptian bazaar. People could experience the sights, sounds, and smells of a Cairo street right there in Paris. Visitors to the Exposition were offered a chance to sample other cultures that many of them might never have otherwise known.

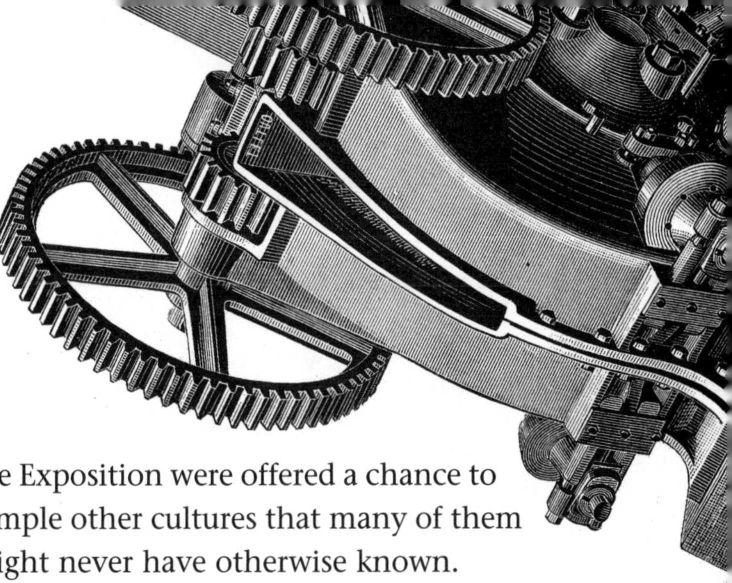

The Palace of Machines, one of the largest and most impressive of the Exposition buildings, housed examples of the very latest in technology. The Palace of Fine Arts, where Rosemary Rita and Gracie went to look for Monsieur Potthast, featured galleries of paintings and sculpture from many countries. As William

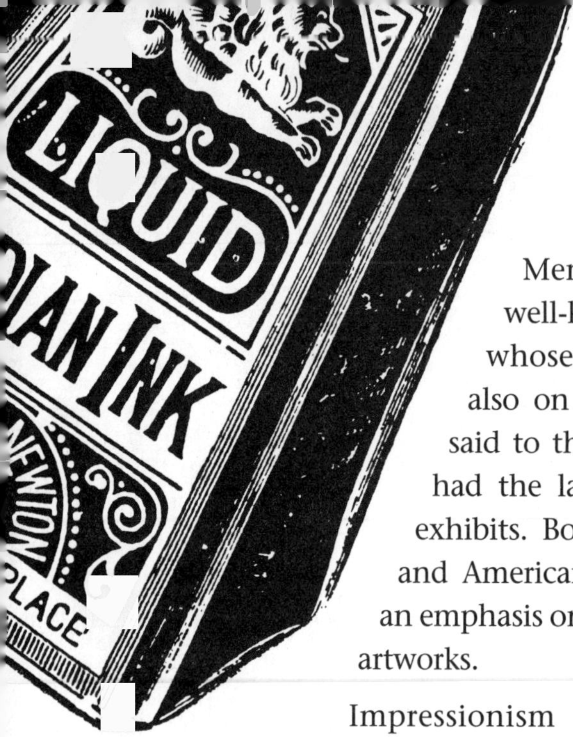

Merritt Chase (a well-known painter whose works were also on exhibit there) said to the girls, France had the largest of these exhibits. Both the French and American galleries put an emphasis on Impressionist artworks.

Impressionism was a major movement in painting (and later, in music) during the late 1800s. It originated in France, and later became popular in the United States. The Impressionist painters were interested in the impression made by a scene they painted. Rather than focusing on making details as "real" as possible, they focused on the effects of light and color. They sometimes used small brush strokes and bright colors to give the impression of light on an object or scene.

Some of the most famous French

ESTERBROOK'S
MAMMOTH FALCON
340

Impressionists were Claude Monet, Pierre Auguste Renoir, and Camille Pisarro. Others who painted in the Impressionist style at different times in their careers were Paul Cezanne and Edgar Degas. Monet, Renoir, and Cezanne were some of the French painters whose work was shown at the Exposition in 1889.

Edward Potthast (1857–1927), an American Impressionist, was among the American painters who had their work exhibited at the Palace of Fine Arts in 1889. He was born in Cincinnati, Ohio, where he received his first training as an artist. By the time Rosemary Rita and Gracie met him, he had spent about six years studying in Europe.

The painting the girls saw in Paris, *A Young Brittany Girl,* was a big success with the art critics at the 1889 Exposition. Edward Potthast was considered a promising young painter, and at the end of 1889 he returned to the United States. He moved to Cincinnati and, later, to New York. He became especially well-known for his paintings of beach scenes. Edward Potthast also made a living as a lithographer and a magazine illustrator. *A Young Brittany Girl* now belongs to the National Museum of American Art in Washington, D.C.

The people who attended the Exposition dressed in fashionable clothes. Men were outfitted in their finest suits and hats, many of them carrying walking sticks. The women wore long dresses, white gloves, and fancy, decorated hats. In 1889, bustles were worn by women under their skirts. Made of either wire or whalebone, they pushed the skirts out in the back so they looked like a camel's hump. Women also wore bustle petticoats, which were made of a stiff material covered with ruffles and pleats. This style had one problem—it was uncomfortable for women to sit down!

Of course, there were souvenirs of all kinds to be purchased at the Exposition. Postcards, for instance! Black-and-white prints or engravings of scenes from the fair were reproduced on cards. There were also postcards with color reproductions and black-and-white scenes tinted with watercolor. Today, postcards from the nineteenth century are valued by collectors, and it is still possible to find them in antique stores, junk stores, or bookshops. Paris is famous for its flea markets, and postcard collectors scour those markets for goodies. If you are interested in old postcards of all kinds, you might try hunting for them at garage sales, flea markets, and used bookstores. Who knows what adventures you might get into?

PARIS ET SES MERVEILLES
406 Avenue des Champs-Élysées et
arc de triomphe de l'Étoile
-la-Bretonnerie, Paris
Reproduction interdite

French Expressions Used in this Book

Excusez-moi. *Ehkss-kew-zay mwah.*	Excuse me.
Merci beaucoup. *Mehr-see-boh-koo.*	Thank you very much.
Au secours! *Ah suh-koor!*	Help!
Comment vous applez vous? *Koh-mahn voo zah-play voo?*	What is your name?
Allons-y! *Ah-lohn-zee!*	Let's go!
Je suis désolé. *Zhuh swee day-zoh-lay.*	I'm sorry.
Magnifique! *Mah-nyee-feek!*	How beautiful!
Mon Dieu! *Mohn-dyuh!*	My goodness!
Ça va. *Sah-vah.*	That's all right.

Other Useful Expressions

Bonsoir. *Bohn-swahr.*	Good evening.
Comprenez-vous? *Kohn-pruh-nay voo?*	Do you understand?
Comment allez-vous? *Koh-mahn tah-lay voo?*	How are you?
C'est combien? *Say kohn-byan?*	How much is it?
Pouvez-vous m'aider s'il vous plait? *Poo-vay voo meh-day seel voo pleh?*	Can you help me?

Generations

Rosemary Ruth "Rosemarie" Berger (Christianson)
Great-great-great-grandmother

Rosemary Grace "Gracie" Christianson (Gibson)
Great-great-grandmother

Rosemary Anna Gibson (Ryan)
Great-grandmother

Rosemary Regina "Mimi" Ryan (Carlisle)
Grandmother

Rosemary "Leigh" Carlisle (Hampton)
Mother

Rosemary Rita Hampton

BORN	AGE 10
1860	1870
1879	1889
1909	1919
1935	1945
1965	1975
1991	2001

About the Author

I have wished many times over the years that my children could have known my grandmother, Mimi. I am thrilled that her spirit comes to life in these books. Now I can share Mimi with my own children and many other children as well.

—BARBARA ROBERTSON

Barbara Robertson lives in Greenville, South Carolina, with her husband, Marsh, and their three children, Ashley, Will, and Eileen. She has earned B.A. and M.A. degrees in Elementary and Early Childhood Education. A former teacher, Barbara enjoys volunteering at her children's schools. In addition, she serves on several community boards (Children's Hospital, Friends of the Greenville Zoo, and the South Carolina Children's Theatre). When she's not pounding on her word processor or chauffeuring her children, you might find Barbara on the tennis court or curled up with a good book.

Photo: Kay Roper

WHAT'S NEXT?

Read a chapter from Rosemary Rita's next adventure at winslowpress.com